Skylite and Gertie

PAGE PUBLISHING
Conneaut Lake, PA

First originally published by Page Publishing 2024

ISBN 979-8-88960-560-7 (pbk)
ISBN 979-8-88960-628-4 (digital)

Skylite and Gertie

The Case of the Stolen Honey

PATTY HAMILL

Hey, Gertie, why are you flying so crazy? asked Skylite.
Oh, Skylight! sobbing Gertie said. Someone is stealing
my honey! I am so upset. Who would do such a thing?
Oh, I think I know, replied Red. I bet it is Ouchie, I heard!
He has been doing this a lot lately.

Oh. HI, Red! Where have you been? asked
Skylite. I have been hiding from Ouchie!
Yeah, I'm pretty sure myself it is Ouchie, spoke Gertie.
We all know it is not, Antsy said as they all chuckled. Poor Antsy.
He tries so hard, but he keeps getting stuck, and we
keep pulling him out.

Where were you hiding, Red? asked Gertie. We all have been
Hiding under leaves in bushes when we hear Ouchie, said Red.

When we hear Ouchie flying by
That is where we go to hide from Ouchie, said Red. We need to do something and stop Ouchie.

Hey, Gertie and Red, you both stay here, and let's check it out! said Skylite.
Skylite flew off and was blinded by the fog rolling in. *Wow*. I can't see hardly anything. Buzzing sounds? Where is the noise coming from?

Approaching the hive, Skylite saw Ouchie.
Frantically Skylite flew off. Gee, I hope he did not see me.
Ouchie sends quivers down my wings.

Waiting patiently, Gertie and Red spotted Skylite
flying out of the dense fog.
Gertie, Red, follow me, and you will see for yourself how mean
Ouchie is! Let's go!! Following Skylite, they approached the
hive.

Oh no! yelled Gertie. It is Ouchie. But why, Ouchie?

Simple, Gertie, spoke Ouchie!

You have the sweetest honey ever. I want it.

Ouchie, you need to stop stealing honey from everyone, replied Red. Red yelled at Ouchie, You need to stop! Who is going to stop me? You, Red? You know what will happen to you if you do. Don't you ever come back here, Red, or else!

You know you can have honey anytime. Just ask for it. Laughing, Ouchie said, Once I get all the honey, I am going to destroy all the hives. No, sobbing Gertie said! Gertie, Red, let's go. We can figure out a plan and outsmart Ouchie.

Red, what did Ouchie mean by that? asked Skylite and Gertie. Red, sobbing, said, That Ouchie pokes us ladybugs with a gel, and we end up becoming zombies.

Zombies! How? asked Gertie and Skylite. They
stand guard over the baby wasps, and we cannot move.
Sobbing Red said, I have seen it done. It is awful. That is why
we hide under leaves, and we can't even go home to our village.
We must not let Ouchie find my village.
Wow, said Skylite and Gertie. We need to do something.

I have a great idea! This will never fail. Number one, we
live in a beautiful forest called Neon. But see I have magical powers.
I will explain my plan as soon as you can get your workers to help.
Meet you back in Neon! Now go!

The excitement of honeybees and ladybugs
gathering together was a magical moment in Neon.
Neon was so special that the only way in was by invitation
by Skylite.

Gertie said, Well, Skylite what is your plan?
Well, here it is. You will be able to switch your wings
only after I sprinkle you with magical dust.

Once you have been dusted, your wings will slide off
to be swapped.
What? Swapped? Yes, replied Skylite. Your wings will be
much stronger.

MAGIC DUST

Here is the plan. Once Gertie's honeybees are ladybugs
They are going to go enter the hive. Once they enter, Ouchie
and his troops are going to try—and I mean *try*—to turn them into
zombies, *but* the real ladybugs that are honeybees will move jars
under the hive and smack his troops on the head, and they all
fall into jars!

Ouchie was frantic because not one bug turned into a zombie.
The more Ouchie's troops try, the more their stingers fall off.
Ouchie flew to Skylight. *What* did you do? I switched the
wings so Gertie can get her hive back and stop you from turning

ladybugs into zombies. Get your own guards. Stop using
the ladybugs.
Skylite how do I get my ouchies back?

In a day or two they will be fine so go and guard them

Afterward go build your own nest. If you need honey just ask Gertie

Skylite, Gertie, and Red were so happy. Gertie had her hive back.
And Red was able to go back home with the rest of his family.

About the Author

I started to write children's books a very long time ago. *Skylite's Adventures* is the book that got me started to write more. I use insects for my characters. I know they are bugs, but we need these bugs for our planet to survive. Each insect has its purpose. Let's take the honeybee for them to pollinate the flowers do we can grow our produce. They make honey. Honey has a lot of benefits. For my lightning bug—every summer, I would wait until it got dark, and all you could see was these tiny lights all over. I used to go out and catch them and then let them go. But not, I am lucky if I see any because of the chemicals that are being used for a greener lawn.

So now when I go outside, I see there is not that many. This is how I wrote *Skylite*—he is my lightning bug, my hero.